Published in 2005 by Simply Read Books Inc.
www.simplyreadbooks.com

Cataloguing in Publication Data

van Turennout, Paola, 1976-
    One little bug / Paola van Turennout.

ISBN 1-894965-12-4

    I.Title.
PS8643.A68O64 2005   jC813'.6   C2004-902815-4

10 9 8 7 6 5 4 3 2 1

Printed in China

Book Design Paola van Turennout www.graphitize.com

This book is dedicated to Donnie.

One Little Bug

By PAOLA VAN TURENNOUT

One little bug
Can be very small.

He's not much to look at,
And not very tall.

But just add another
And now you have two,

That's twice as many
To keep bugging you.

Add two to the pair
And now you have four,

But three at that height
Seem afraid of the floor.

To make it to five,
Add one to the scene,

That makes enough
For a basketball team.

Then to make seven,
Just add two more fellas.

Now that it's raining
Let's add an umbrella.

One more on top
Makes eight, but now see,

Two little snails
Want to watch some TV.

The six that are left
Need to reorganize,

While they try not to step
In each other's eyes.

Joining the group
Are some curious bees.

Nine gets quite tippy –
So nobody sneeze!

Now one tiny flea
Has landed on top,

And then all ten bugs
Start to wobble and flop.

Look out – they're falling!
The poor little things!

They all should go home
Before bedtime begins.

As the bees race back home
They buzz by some cars,

Which are stuck in the traffic,
And not moving far.

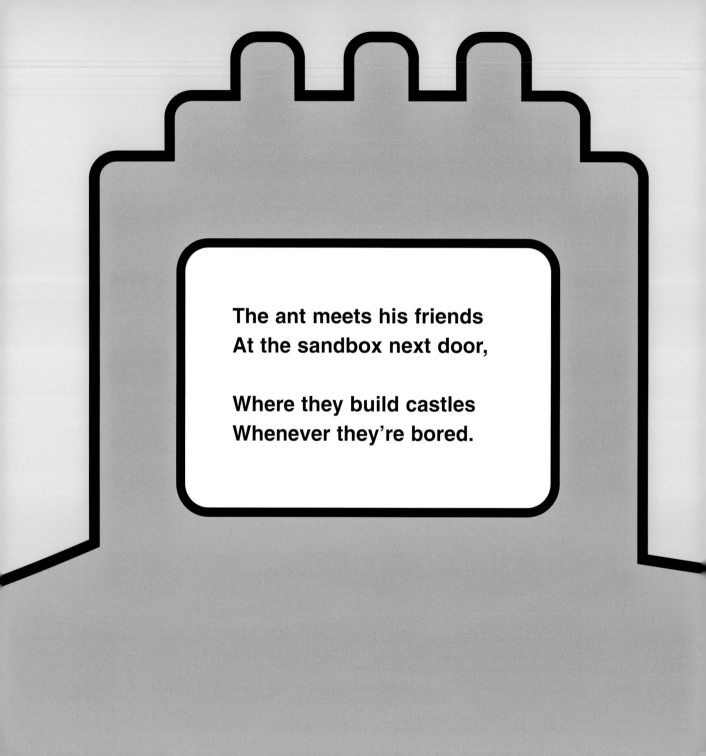

The ant meets his friends
At the sandbox next door,

Where they build castles
Whenever they're bored.

The flea has a home
Still stranger than that.

She lives on a bunny
Who pops out of a hat!

The spider goes home
To a corner from where,

He'll hang out and wait
To give you a scare!

The worms go home
To the compost heap.

That leaves the first bug –
But where will he sleep?

That little bug
Will just wait in this nook,

To be here the next time
You open this book.